This
Treasure Cove Story
belongs to

D0475613

ONWARD

A CENTUM BOOK 978-1-913865-23-8
Published in Great Britain by Centum Books Ltd.
This edition published 2021.

1 3 5 7 9 10 8 6 4 2

© 2021 Disney Enterprises, Inc. and Pixar.
All rights reserved.

No part of this publication may be reproduced, stored in a retrieval
system, or transmitted in any form or by any means, electronic,
mechanical, photocopying, recording or otherwise without
the prior permission of the publishers.

Centum Books Ltd, 20 Devon Square, Newton Abbot,
Devon, TQ12 2HR, UK.

www.centumbooksltd.co.uk | books@centumbooksltd.co.uk
CENTUM BOOKS LIMTED. Reg. No. 07641486.

A CIP catalogue record for this book is available
from the British Library.

Printed in China.

MIX
Paper from
responsible sources
FSC® C149078
FSC
www.fsc.org

A Treasure Cove Story

FROM THE MOVIE

Disney · PIXAR
ONWARD

Adapted by
Courtney Carbone

Illustrated by
Nick Balian
and the Disney Storybook Art Team

Designed by
Tony Fejeran

Long ago, the world was full of wonder! Unicorns soared through the sky, merfolk frolicked in the oceans and centaurs raced through the forests. Everyone used magic to make their lives easier.

But in time, technology took over. Magic slowly **faded away**...

Now in the town of
New Mushroomton,
life was ordinary.

A teenage elf named **Ian Lightfoot** lived
there with his mum, **Laurel**, his older brother,
Barley and their pet dragon, **Blazey**.

K101.7

On Ian's sixteenth birthday, Laurel gave him a special gift that changed everything. Ian's father, who had passed away before Ian was born, had left it for him. It was a **wizard's staff**, a **Phoenix Gem** and a **spell** that could bring his father back to life for one day!

Ian had always wanted to **meet his dad** more than anything and now he would have the chance.

Barley thought he was an expert at magic.

He tried to conjure their father over and over again, but nothing worked. When Ian tried, the boys' father slowly began to **appear**. The brothers couldn't believe it!

Ian, not Barley, had the **gift of magic**!

Then something
went wrong – the
Phoenix Gem
exploded before
Ian finished the spell!
All that appeared of their
father were his **legs**!

The brothers had to act fast – their dad would **disappear forever** at sunset the next day. They jumped into Barley's van, **Guinevere**, to set off on a quest to find another Phoenix Gem.

They arrived at the **Manticore's Tavern**. Barley believed that the legendary Manticore, known for her life of danger and risk, could give them a map to another gem. With their dad in disguise, the group entered the tavern...

...and saw that it was no longer a place of **adventure** and **danger**. It was a fun family restaurant!

The boys found the Manticore and asked for the map to the Phoenix Gem. She refused, telling them that the journey was **far too risky**. She offered them a children's menu instead, since it was based on her map.

Ian pointed out to the Manticore that she wasn't the daring creature she used to be. The Manticore realised the truth in his words. Enraged, she began to **destroy** parts of the tavern and her map was destroyed, too!

As the building crumbled around them, Ian used magic to **save their dad** from a falling beam!

Without a map, Ian and Barley decided to follow the children's menu and go to a place called **Raven's Point**.

On the way there, Guinevere ran out of petrol. Ian tried to use magic to make the petrol can bigger, but he **shrank Barley** instead!

At a nearby petrol station, the boys accidentally angered a motorcycle club of sprites called the **Pixie Dusters**. **The sprites chased them!**

The trio ran to the van. Ian was afraid to drive, but with Barley's help, he weaved and swerved all over the motorway, leaving the Pixie Dusters behind!

Then the police pulled the van over. The brothers tricked them by using magic to disguise themselves as their mum's boyfriend, **Officer Colt Bronco**.

After the boys got away, they began to argue. Ian was worried about **wasting time** and Barley wanted Ian to listen to his ideas.

All of a sudden, their dad started **dancing** and got the boys to join in!

Ian finally agreed to do things Barley's way, so they left the motorway and drove down an ancient road called the **Path of Peril**. It led to a cliff overlooking a bottomless pit! The only way to get across the pit was with magic.

With Barley's **encouragement**, Ian made it to the other side. He lowered a bridge for everyone to cross.

Suddenly, the police, including the real Officer Colt Bronco, **were on their tail**!

Barley had to **sacrifice** Guinevere to buy some time to get away. He placed a rock on the van's accelerator and watched as she crashed into some rocks, blocking the road.

They continued on foot and realised they needed to follow the path the **ravens** were pointing out. They found one statue…

which pointed them to **another** statue…

which finally led them to a river flowing into a **dark cave**.

With magic, Ian created a **cheese-puff boat** so they could speed along the river. Barley said he regretted not saying goodbye to their dad before he died. That was when he'd decided never to be scared again.

At the end of the tunnel, the trio came to a set of stairs and an ancient archway. They ran to safety, dodging some **dangerous traps**!

They finally reached the end of their quest – only to find themselves right back in New Mushroomton! Ian was angry that he had trusted Barley. He stormed off with their dad. They were almost **out of time**!

Alone with his thoughts, Ian **realised** that everything he wanted to do with his dad, he'd already done with Barley.

His older brother had **always been there for him**.

Meanwhile, Barley had found the Phoenix Gem, but he had also awakened a **CURSE**! Ian returned and saw his high school transform into a dragon!

Just then, the Manticore and Laurel swooped in. They had **teamed up** to help the boys. While they fought the dragon, Ian tried to bring back the rest of his dad.

But before long, the dragon charged at Ian and Barley! Ian wanted to give Barley his **last chance** to say goodbye to their dad. Using magic, he sent the Manticore's sword, the Curse Crusher, deep into the monster's core, defeating it once and for all!

Rocks and rubble fell all around
Ian. He watched from afar as Barley
and their dad, now in full form,
talked and laughed together.
The two shared a final embrace before
their father disappeared into thin air.

When the brothers reunited, Barley told Ian that their dad was **very proud** of them. And he had asked Barley to give Ian a big, loving hug.

Ian smiled. Even though he hadn't met his dad, the quest had brought him closer to Barley. He knew he could always depend on his **big brother**.

Treasure Cove Stories

Please contact Centum Books to receive the full list of titles in the *Treasure Cove Stories* series.
books@centumbooksltd.co.uk

*Book list may be subject to change. Not all titles are listed.